RAINBOW magic

RUBY THE RED FAIRY
1-84362-016-2

AMBER THE ORANGE FAIRY
1-84362-017-0

SAFFRON THE YELLOW FAIRY
1-84362-018-9

FERN THE GREEN FAIRY
1-84362-019-7

SKY THE BLUE FAIRY
1-84362-020-0

IZZY THE INDIGO FAIRY
1-84362-021-9

HEATHER THE VIOLET FAIRY
1-84362-022-7

Collect all seven Rainbow Magic
books to bring the sparkle
back to Fairyland...

Dedicated to Fiona Waters,
who has loved fairies
all her life

Special thanks to
Narinder Dhami

ORCHARD BOOKS
338 Euston Road, London NW1 3BH
Hachette Children's Books
Orchard Books Australia
Level 17/207 Kent Street, Sydney, NSW 2000
A Paperback Original
First published in Great Britain in 2003 as 1 84362 017 0
Text © Working Partners Limited 2003
Created by Working Partners Limited, London W6 0QT
Illustrations © Georgie Ripper 2003
The right of Georgie Ripper to be identified as the illustrator
of this work has been asserted by her in accordance
with the Copyright, Designs and Patents Act, 1988.
A CIP catalogue record for this book is available
from the British Library.
ISBN 1 84616 323 4
1 3 5 7 9 10 8 6 4 2
Printed in Great Britain

Amber
the Orange
Fairy

by Daisy Meadows

illustrated by Georgie Ripper

ORCHARD BOOKS

The Fairyland Palace

Maze

Forest

Orchard

Black Pot

Meadow

Tower

Beach

Rockpools

Rainspell Island

Shells

Jack Frost's
Ice Castle

Tom Goodfellow's
House

Merry-go-round

Willow
Tree

Mrs Merry's
Cottage

Stream

Field

Town

Mermaid
Cottage

Harbour

Dolphin Cottage

Cold winds blow and thick ice form,
I conjure up this fairy storm.
To seven corners of the mortal world
the Rainbow Fairies will be hurled!

I curse every part of Fairyland,
with a frosty wave of my icy hand.
For now and always, from this fateful day,
Fairyland will be cold and grey!

Ruby is safely hidden in the
pot-at-the-end-of-the-rainbow.
Now Rachel and Kirsty must find
Amber the Orange Fairy

Contents

A Very Unusual Shell

"What a lovely day!" Rachel Walker shouted, staring up at the blue sky. She and her friend, Kirsty Tate, were running along Rainspell Island's yellow, sandy beach. Their parents walked a little way behind them.

"It's a *magical* day," Kirsty added. The two friends smiled at each other.

Rachel and Kirsty had come to Rainspell Island for their holidays. They had soon found out it really *was* a magical place!

As they run, they passed rock pools that shone like jewels in the sunshine.

Rachel spotted a little *splash!* in one of the pools. "There's something in there, Kirsty!" she pointed. "Let's go and look."

The girls jogged over to the pool and crouched down to see.

Kirsty's heart thumped as she gazed into the crystal clear water. "What is it?" she asked.

Suddenly, the water rippled. A little brown crab scuttled sideways across the sandy bottom and vanished under a rock.

Kirsty felt disappointed. "I thought it might be another Rainbow Fairy," she said.

"So did I, "Rachel sighed. "Never mind. We'll keep on looking."

"Of course we will," Kirsty agreed. Then she put hcr finger to her lips as their parents came up behind them. "*Ssh.*"

Kirsty and Rachel had a big secret. They were helping to find the Rainbow Fairies. Thanks to Jack Frost's wicked spell, the fairies were lost on Rainspell Island. And until they were all found there would be no colour in Fairyland.

Rachel looked at the shimmering blue sea. "Shall we have a swim?" she asked.

But Kirsty wasn't listening. She was shading her eyes with her hand and looking further along the beach. "Over there, Rachel — by those rocks," she said.

Then Rachel could see it too — something winking and sparkling in the sunshine. "Wait for me!" she called, as Kirsty hurried over there.

When they saw what it was, the two
friends sighed in disappointment.

"It's just the wrapper from a
chocolate bar," Rachel said sadly. She
bent down and picked up the shiny
purple foil.

Kirsty thought for a moment. "Do you remember what the Fairy Queen said?" she asked.

Rachel nodded. "*Let the magic come to you*," she said. "You're right, Kirsty. We should just enjoy our holiday, and wait for the magic to happen. After all, that's how we found Ruby in the pot-at-the-end-of-the-rainbow, isn't it?" She put down her beach bag on the sand. "Come on – race you into the sea!"

They rushed into the water. The sea was cold and salty, but the sun felt warm on their backs. They waved at their parents, sitting on the sand, and splashed about in the waves until they got goosebumps.

"Ow!" Kirsty gasped as they paddled out of the water. "I just stood on something sharp."

"It might have been a shell," said Rachel. "There are lots of them round here." She picked up a pale pink one and showed it to Kirsty.

"Let's see how many we can find," Kirsty said.

The two girls walked along the beach looking for shells. They found long, thin, blue shells and tiny, round, white shells.

Soon their hands were full. They had walked right round the curve of the bay. Rachel looked over her shoulder and a sudden gust of wind whipped her hair across her face. "Look how far we've come," she said. Kirsty stopped. The wind tugged at her T-shirt and made goosebumps stand out on her arms. "It's getting cold now," she said. "Shall we go back?" "Yes, it must be nearly teatime," said Rachel.

The two girls began to walk back along the beach. They'd only gone a few steps when the wind suddenly dropped again.

"That's funny," said Kirsty. "It's not windy here."

They looked back and saw little swirls of sand being blown in the wind where they'd just been. "Oh!" said Rachel, and the two friends looked at each other with excitement.

"It's magic," Kirsty whispered. "It *has* to be!"

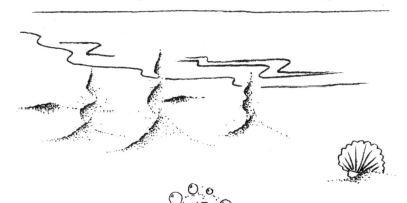

They walked back and the breeze swirled around their legs again. Then the golden sand at their feet began to drift gently to one side, as if invisible hands were pushing it away. A large scallop shell appeared, much bigger than the other shells on the beach. It was pearly white with soft orange streaks, and it was tightly closed.

Quickly the girls knelt down on the sand, spilling the little shells out of their hands. Kirsty was just about to pick up the scallop shell when Rachel put out her hand. "Listen," she whispered.

They both listened hard.

There it was again.

Inside the shell, a tiny, silvery voice hummed softly...

The Magic Feather

Very carefully, Rachel picked up the shell. It felt warm and smooth.

The humming stopped at once. "I mustn't be scared," said the tiny voice. "I just have to be brave, and help will come very soon."

Hummm...

Kirsty put her face close to the shell. "Hello," she whispered. "Is there a fairy in there?"

"Yes!" cried the voice. "I'm Amber the *Orange* Fairy! Can you get me out of here?"

"Of course we will," Kirsty promised. "My name is Kirsty, and my friend Rachel is here too." She looked up at Rachel, her eyes shining. "We've found another Rainbow Fairy!"

"Quick," Rachel said. "Let's get the shell open." She took hold of the scallop shell and tried to pull the two halves apart. Nothing happened.

"Try again," said Kirsty. She and Rachel each grasped one half of the shell and tugged. But the shell stayed tightly shut.

"What's happening?" Amber called. She sounded worried.

"We can't open the shell," Kirsty said. "But we'll think of something." She turned to Rachel. "If we find a piece of driftwood, maybe we could use it to open the shell."

Rachel glanced around the beach. "I can't see any driftwood," she said. "We could try tapping the shell on a rock."

"But that might hurt Amber," Kirsty pointed out.

Suddenly Rachel remembered
something. "What about the magic bags
the Fairy Queen gave us?" she said.

"Of course!" Kirsty cried. She put her
face close to the shell again.
"Amber, we're going to
look in our magic
bags," she said.
"OK, but please
hurry," Amber called.
Rachel opened her
beach bag. The two
magic bags were hidden
under her towel. One of the bags
was glowing with a golden light.
Carefully, Rachel pulled it out.
"Look," she whispered to Kirsty. "This
one is all lit up."

"Open it, quick," Kirsty whispered back.

As Rachel undid the bag, a fountain
of glittering sparks flew out.

"What's inside?" Kirsty asked, her
eyes wide.

Rachel slid her hand into the bag.
She could feel something light
and soft. She pulled it out,
scattering sparkles
everywhere.
It was a
shimmering
golden
feather.

Kirsty and Rachel stared at the feather.

"It's really pretty," said Kirsty. "But what are we going to *do* with it?"

"I don't know," Rachel replied. She tried to use the feather to push the two halves of the shell apart. But the feather just curled up in her hand. "Maybe we should ask Amber."

"Amber, we've looked in the magic bags," Kirsty said, "and we've found a feather."

"Oh, good!" Amber said happily from inside the shell.

"But we don't know what to do with it," Rachel added.

Amber laughed. It sounded like the tinkle of a tiny bell. "You tickle the shell, of course!" she said.

"Do you think that will work?" Rachel said to Kirsty.

"Let's give it a try," Kirsty said.

Rachel began to tickle the shell with the feather. At first nothing happened. Then they heard a soft, gritty chuckle. Then another and another. Slowly the two halves of the shell began to open.

"It's working," Kirsty gasped. "Keep tickling, Rachel!"

The shell was laughing hard now. The two halves opened wider...

And there, sitting inside the smooth, peach-coloured shell, was Amber the Orange Fairy.

A Stranger in the Pot

"I'm free!" Amber cried joyfully.

She shot out of the shell and up into the air, her wings fluttering in a rainbow-coloured blur. Orange fairy dust floated down around Kirsty and Rachel. It turned into orange bubbles as it fell. One of the bubbles landed on Rachel's arm and burst with a tiny POP!

"The bubbles smell like oranges!"
Rachel smiled.

Amber spun through the sky, turning
cartwheels one after the other. "Thank
you!" she called. Then she swooped
down towards Rachel and Kirsty.

She wore a shiny orange catsuit and
long boots. Her flame-coloured hair
was held in a high ponytail, tied with a
band of peach blossoms. In her hand
was an orange wand tipped with gold.

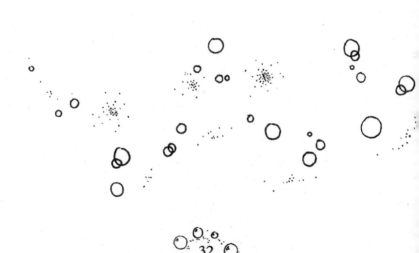

"I'm so glad you found me!" Amber shouted. She landed on Rachel's shoulder, then cartwheeled lightly across to Kirsty's. "But who are you? And where are my Rainbow sisters? And what's happening in Fairyland? How am I going to get back there?"

Kirsty and Rachel couldn't get a word in.

Suddenly, Amber stopped. She floated down and landed softly on Rachel's hand. "I'm sorry," she said with a smile. "But I haven't had anyone to talk to. I've been shut up in this shell ever since Jack Frost's spell banished us from Fairyland. How did you know where to find me?"

"Kirsty and I promised your sister Ruby that we would look for all the Rainbow Fairies," Rachel told her.

"Ruby?" Amber's face lit up. She spun round on Rachel's hand. "You've found Ruby?"

"Yes, she's quite safe," Rachel said. "She's in the pot-at-the-end-of-the-rainbow."

Amber did a joyful backflip. "Please take me to her!" she begged.

"I'll ask our parents if we can go for a walk," Kirsty said. And she ran off across the beach.

"Do you know what is happening in Fairyland?" Amber asked Rachel.

Rachel nodded. She and Kirsty had flown with Ruby to Fairyland. Ruby had shrunk them to fairy size and given them fairy wings. "King Oberon and Queen Titania miss you very much," Rachel told Amber. "With no colour, Fairyland is a sad place."

Amber's wings drooped.

Kirsty was hurrying back towards them. "Mum said we can go for a walk," she panted.

"Well, what are we waiting for? Let's go!" Amber called. She flew up and did a somersault in mid-air.

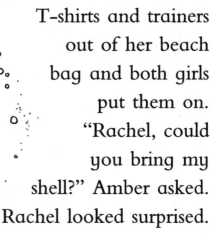

Rachel pulled their shorts, T-shirts and trainers out of her beach bag and both girls put them on. "Rachel, could you bring my shell?" Amber asked. Rachel looked surprised. "Yes, if you want," she said.

Amber nodded. "It's really comfy," she explained. "It will make a lovely bed for me and my sisters."

Rachel put the shell in her beach bag, and they set off, with Amber sitting cross-legged on Kirsty's shoulder.

"My wings are a bit stiff after being in the shell," she told them. "I don't think I can fly very far yet."

The girls followed the path to the clearing in the wood where the pot-at-the-end-of-the-rainbow was hidden.

"Here we are," said Rachel. "The pot is over there." She stopped. The pot was where they'd left it, under the weeping willow tree. But climbing out of it was a big, green frog.

"Oh no!" Rachel gasped. She and Kirsty stared at the frog in horror. Where was Ruby?

Home Sweet Home

Rachel dashed forward and grabbed the frog round his plump, green tummy.

The frog turned his head and glared at her, his eyes bulging. "And what do you think *you're* doing?" he croaked.

Rachel was so shocked, she let go of the frog. He hopped away from her, looking very annoyed.

"It's a talking frog!" Kirsty gasped,
her eyes wide. "And it looks like it's
wearing glasses..."

"Bertram!" Amber flew down from
Kirsty's shoulder. "I didn't know it was
you."

Bertram bowed his head as Amber
hugged him. "Thank goodness you're
safe, Miss Amber!" he said happily.
"And may I say, it's very good to see
you again."

Amber beamed at Rachel and Kirsty. "Bertram isn't an ordinary frog, you know," she explained. "He's one of King Oberon's footmen."

"Oh, yes!" said Kirsty. "I remember now. We saw the frog footmen when we went to Fairyland with Ruby."

"But they were wearing purple uniforms then," Rachel added.

"Excuse me, Miss, but a frog in a purple uniform would *not* be a good idea on Rainspell Island," Bertram pointed out. "It's much better if I look like an ordinary frog."

"But what are you doing here, Bertram?" asked Amber. "And where's Ruby?"

"Don't worry, Miss Amber," Bertram replied. "Miss Ruby is safe in the pot." He suddenly looked very stern. "King Oberon sent me to Rainspell. The Cloud Fairies spotted Jack Frost's goblins sneaking out of Fairyland. We think he has sent them here to stop the Rainbow Fairies being found."

Kirsty felt a shiver run down her spine. "Jack Frost's goblins?" she said.

"They're his servants," Amber explained. Her wings trembled and she looked very scared. "They'd rather keep Fairyland cold and grey!"

"Never fear, Miss Amber," Bertram croaked. "I'll look after you."

Suddenly a shower of red fairy dust shot out of the pot. Ruby fluttered out. "I heard voices," she shouted joyfully. "Amber! I *knew* it was you!"

"Ruby!" Amber called. And she cartwheeled through the air towards her sister.

Rachel and Kirsty watched as the two
fairies flew into each other's arms. The
air around them fizzed with tiny red
flowers and orange bubbles.

"Thank you, Kirsty and Rachel," said Ruby. She and Amber floated down to them, holding hands. "It's so good to have Amber back safely."

"What about you?" Rachel asked. "Have you been all right in the pot?"

Ruby nodded. "I'm fine now that Bertram is here," she replied. "And I've been making the pot into a fairy home."

"I've brought my shell with me," Amber said. "It will make a lovely bed for us. Show her, Rachel."

Rachel put her bag down on the grass and took the creamy orange shell out of it.

"It's beautiful," said Ruby. Then she smiled at Rachel and Kirsty. "Would you like to come and see our new home?" she asked.

"But the pot's too small for Kirsty and me to get inside," Rachel began. Then she began to tingle with excitement. "Are you going to make us fairy size again?"

Ruby nodded. She and Amber flew over the girls' heads, showering them with fairy dust. Rachel and Kirsty started to shrink, just as they had done before. Soon they were tiny, the same size as Ruby and Amber.

"I *love* being a fairy," Kirsty said happily. She twisted round to look at her silvery wings.

"Me too," Rachel agreed. She was getting used to seeing flowers as tall as trees!

Bertram hopped over to the pot. "I'll wait outside," he croaked.

"Come this way," said Ruby. She took Rachel's hand, and Amber took Kirsty's. Then the fairies led them towards the pot.

Rachel and Kirsty fluttered through the air, dodging a butterfly that was as big as they were. Its wings felt like velvet as they brushed gently past it.

"I'm getting better at flying!" Kirsty laughed as she landed neatly on the edge of the pot. She looked down eagerly.

The pot was full of sunlight. There were little chairs made from twigs tied with blades of grass. Each chair had a cushion made from a soft red berry. Rugs of bright green leaves covered the floor.

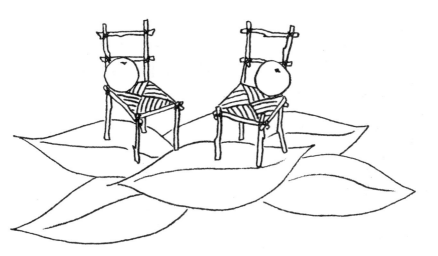

"Shall we bring in the shell?" asked Rachel.

The others thought this was a very good idea. When they flew out of the pot, Bertram was already pushing the shell across the grass towards them.

"Here you are," he croaked.

The shell seemed very heavy now
that Rachel and Kirsty were the same
size as Ruby and Amber. But Bertram
helped them to heave it into the pot.

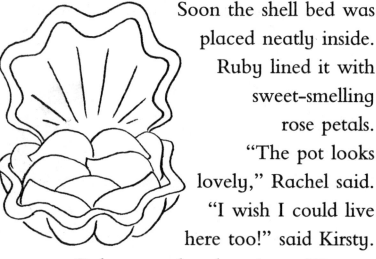

Soon the shell bed was
placed neatly inside.
Ruby lined it with
sweet-smelling
rose petals.

"The pot looks
lovely," Rachel said.

"I wish I could live
here too!" said Kirsty.

Ruby turned to her sister. "Do *you*
like it, Amber?" she asked.

"It's beautiful," Amber replied. "It
reminds me of our house back in
Fairyland. I wish I could see Fairyland
again. I miss it so much."

Ruby smiled. "Well, I can show you Fairyland," she said, "even though we can't go back there yet. Follow me."

Bertram was still on guard next to the pot when they flew out again. "Where are you going, Miss Ruby?" he croaked.

"To the magic pond," Ruby replied. "Come with us." She sprinkled her magic dust over Rachel and Kirsty. Quickly they grew back to their normal size.

They went over to the pond. Ruby flew above the water, scattering fairy dust. Just as before, a picture began to appear. "Fairyland!" Amber cried, gazing into the water. Rachel and Kirsty watched too.

Fairyland still looked sad and chilly. The palace, the toadstool houses, the flowers and the trees were all drab and grey.

Suddenly a cold breeze rippled the surface of the water, and the picture began to fade.

"What's happening?" Kirsty whispered.

Everyone stared down at the pond.
Another picture was taking shape – a
thin, grinning face with frosty white
hair and icicles hanging from his beard.

"Jack Frost!" Ruby gasped in horror.
As she spoke, the air turned icy cold
and the edges of the pool began to
freeze.

"What's happening?" Rachel asked, shivering.

Bertram hopped forward. "This is bad news," he said. "It means that Jack Frost's goblins are close by!"

Goblin Alert!

Rachel and Kirsty felt shivers run down their spine as the whole pond froze over. Jack Frost's grinning face faded away.

"Follow me," ordered Bertram. He hopped over to a large bush. "We'll hide here."

"Maybe we should go back to the pot," said Ruby.

"Not if the goblins are close by," Bertram replied. "We mustn't let them know where the pot is."

The two girls crouched down behind the bush next to Bertram. Ruby and Amber sat very still on Kirsty's shoulder. It was getting colder and colder. Rachel and Kirsty couldn't stop their teeth chattering.

"What are the goblins like?" Rachel asked.

"They're bigger than us," said Amber. She was trembling with fright.

"And they have ugly faces and hooked noses and big feet," Ruby added, holding her sister's hand for comfort.

"Hush, Miss Ruby," Bertram croaked. "I can hear something."

Rachel and Kirsty listened. Suddenly, Rachel saw a hook-nosed shadow flit across the clearing towards them. She grabbed Kirsty's arm. They were peering out of the bush when the leaves rustled right next to them. They almost jumped out of their skin.

"Oi!" said a gruff voice, sounding very close. "What do you think you're doing?" Rachel and Kirsty held their breath.

"Nothing," said another gruff voice, rudely.

"Goblins!" Amber whispered in Kirsty's ear.

"You stood on my toe," said the first goblin crossly.

"No, I didn't," snapped the other goblin.

"Yes, you did! Keep your big feet to yourself!"

"Well, at least my nose isn't as big as yours!"

The bush shook even more. It sounded as if the goblins were pushing and shoving each other.

"Get out of my way!" one of them shouted. "Ow!"

"That'll teach you to push *me*!" yelled the other one.

Rachel and Kirsty looked at each other in alarm. What if the goblins found them there?

"Come on," puffed one of the goblins. "Jack Frost will be really cross if we don't find these fairies. You know he wants us to stop them getting back to Fairyland."

"Well, they're not here, are they?" grumbled the other. "Let's try somewhere else."

The voices died away. The leaves stopped rustling. And suddenly the air felt warm again. There was a cracking sound as the frozen pond began to melt.

"They've gone," Bertram croaked. "Quick, we must get back to the pot."

They all hurried across the clearing. The pot stood under the weeping willow tree, just as before.

"I'll stay outside in case the goblins come back," Bertram began. But a shout from Kirsty stopped them all in their tracks.

"Look!" she cried. "The pot's frozen over!"

Kirsty was right. The top of the pot was covered with a thick sheet of ice. No one, not even a fairy, could get inside.

Bertram to the Rescue

"Oh no!" Ruby gasped. "The goblins must have passed really close. Thank goodness they didn't discover the pot."

She flew over to the pot with Amber right behind her. They drummed on the ice with their tiny fists. But it was too thick for them to break through.

"Shall *we* try, Rachel?" asked Kirsty. "Maybe we could smash the ice with a stick."

But Bertram had another idea. "Stand back, please, everyone," he said.

The girls moved to the edge of the clearing. Ruby sat on Kirsty's hand, and Amber flew over to Rachel. They all watched.

Suddenly, Bertram leaped forward with a mighty hop. He jumped straight at the sheet of ice, kicking out with his webbed feet. But the ice did not break. "Let's try again," he panted.

He jumped forward
again and hit the ice.
This time, there was a
loud cracking sound.
One more jump, and
the ice shattered into
little pieces. Some of it
fell inside the pot. Rachel
and Kirsty rushed over to fish
out these bits before they melted.

"There you are," Bertram croaked.

"Thank you, Bertram," Ruby called.
She and Amber flew down and hugged
the frog.

Bertram looked pleased. "Just doing
my job, Miss Ruby," he said. "You and
Miss Amber must stay very close to the
pot from now on. It's dangerous for
you to go too far."

"We've got to say
goodbye to our friends
first," Amber told him.
She flew into the air and
did a backflip, smiling at
Rachel and Kirsty. "Thank you
a thousand times."

"We'll see you again soon," said
Rachel.

"When we've found your next
Rainbow sister," Kirsty added.

"Good luck!" said Ruby. "We'll be
waiting here for you. Come on,
Amber." She took her
sister's hand, and they
flew over to the pot.
The two fairies turned
to wave at the girls.
Then they disappeared inside.

"Don't worry," Bertram said. "I'll look after them."

"We know you will," Rachel said, as she picked up her beach bag. She and Kirsty walked out of the wood. "I'm glad Ruby isn't on her own any more," said Rachel. "Now she's got Amber *and* Bertram."

"I didn't like those goblins," Kirsty said with a shudder. "I hope they don't come back again."

They made their way back to the beach. Their parents were packing away their towels. Rachel's dad saw Rachel and Kirsty coming down the lane and went to meet them. "You've been a long time," he smiled. "We were just coming to look for you."

"Are we going home now?" Rachel asked.

Mr Walker nodded. "It's very strange," he said. "It's suddenly turned quite chilly."

As he spoke, a cold breeze swirled around Rachel and Kirsty. They shivered and looked up at the sky. The sun had disappeared behind a thick, black cloud. The trees swayed in the wind, and the leaves rustled as if they were whispering to each other.

"Jack Frost's goblins are still here!" Kirsty gasped.

"You're right," Rachel agreed. "Let's hope Bertram can keep Ruby and Amber safe while we look for the other Rainbow Fairies."

RAINBOW
magic

Ruby and Amber have
been rescued. Now it's
time to search for

Saffron the Yellow Fairy

A Very Fierce Bee

"Over here, Kirsty!" called Rachel
Walker. Kirsty ran down one of the
emerald green fields that covered this
part of Rainspell Island. Buttercups and
daisies dotted the grass.

"Don't go too far!" Kirsty's mum called.
She and Kirsty's dad were climbing over
a stile at the top of the field.

Kirsty caught up with her friend. "What have you found, Rachel? Is it another Rainbow Fairy?" she asked hopefully.

"I don't know." Rachel was standing on the bank of a rippling stream. "I thought I heard something."

Kirsty's face lit up. "Maybe there's a fairy in the stream?"

Rachel nodded. She knelt down on the soft grass and put her ear close to the water.

Kirsty crouched down too, and listened really hard.

The sun glittered on the water as it splashed over big, shiny pebbles. Tiny rainbows flashed and sparkled – red, orange, yellow, green, blue, indigo, and violet.

And then they heard a tiny bubbling voice. "Follow me..." it gurgled. "Follow me..."

"Oh!" Rachel gasped. "Did you hear that?"

"Yes," said Kirsty, her eyes wide. "It must be a *magic* stream!"

Rachel felt her heart beat fast. "Maybe the stream will lead us to the Yellow Fairy," she said.

Rachel and Kirsty had a special secret. They had promised the King and Queen of Fairyland they would find the lost Rainbow Fairies. Jack Frost's spell had hidden the Rainbow Fairies on Rainspell Island. Fairyland would be cold and grey until all seven fairies had been found and returned to their home.

Silver fish darted in and out of the bright green weed at the bottom of the stream. "Follow us, follow us..." they whispered in tinkling voices.

Rachel and Kirsty smiled at each other. Titania, the Fairy Queen, had said that the magic would find them!

Kirsty's parents had stopped to admire the stream too. "Which way now?" asked Mr Tate. "You two seem to know where you're going."

"Let's go this way," Kirsty said, pointing along the bank.

A brilliant blue kingfisher flew up from its perch on a twig. Butterflies as bright as jewels fluttered amongst the reeds.

"Everything on Rainspell Island is so beautiful," said Kirsty's mum. "I'm glad we still have five days of holiday left!"

Yes, Rachel thought, and five
Rainbow Fairies still to find: Saffron,
Fern, Sky, Izzy – and Heather!

Read the rest of

Saffron the Yellow Fairy
to find out where the magic stream
leads Rachel and Kirsty.

RAINBOW magic

by Daisy Meadows

Ruby the Red Fairy   ISBN   1 84362 016 2

She's all alone on Rainspell Island...until Rachel and Kirsty promise to track down her Rainbow sisters.

Amber the Orange Fairy   ISBN   1 84362 017 0

She's trapped tight in an unusual place. Can a fluffy feather help rescue her?

Saffron the Yellow Fairy   ISBN   1 84362 018 9

She's stuck in a very sticky situation. How will Rachel and Kirsty free her?

Fern the Green Fairy   ISBN   1 84362 019 7

She's lost in a leafy hollow. And there's a secret to solve to save her.

Sky the Blue Fairy   ISBN   1 84362 020 0

She's having some bubble trouble. Can the rainbow-coloured crab help?

Izzy the Indigo Fairy   ISBN   1 84362 021 9

She's up to her usual mischief. Rachel and Kirsty must get her back to the pot...before it's too late.

Heather the Violet Fairy   ISBN   1 84362 022 7

She's in a spin. Until the colourful carousel horses rush to her rescue.

All priced at £3.99

Rainbow Magic books are available from all good bookshops,
or can be ordered direct from the publisher.
Orchard Books, PO BOX 29, Douglas IM99 1BQ
Credit card orders please telephone 01624 836000
or fax 01624 837033 or visit our Internet site: www.wattspub.co.uk
or e-mail: bookshop@enterprise.net for details.

To order please quote title, author and ISBN
and your full name and address.
Cheques and postal orders should be made payable to 'Bookpost plc.'
Postage and packing is FREE within the UK
(overseas customers should add £1.00 per book).

Prices and availability are subject to change.

FERN THE GREEN FAIRY
1-84362-019-7

SAFFRON THE YELLOW FAIRY
1-84362-018-9

AMBER THE ORANGE FAIRY
1-84362-017-0

RUBY THE RED FAIRY
1-84362-016-2

HEATHER THE VIOLET FAIRY
1-84362-022-7

IZZY THE INDIGO FAIRY
1-84362-021-9

SKY THE BLUE FAIRY
1-84362-020-0

Collect all seven Rainbow Magic
books to bring the sparkle
back to Fairyland...

Dedicated to Joanna Pilkington,
who found fairies in her
beautiful garden

Special thanks to
Narinder Dhami

ORCHARD BOOKS
338 Euston Road, London NW1 3BH
Hachette Children's Books
Orchard Books Australia
Level 17/207 Kent Street, Sydney, NSW 2000
A Paperback Original
First published in Great Britain in 2003 as 1 84362 016 2
Text © Working Partners Limited 2003
Created by Working Partners Limited, London W6 0QT
Illustrations © Georgie Ripper 2003
The right of Georgie Ripper to be identified as the illustrator
of this work has been asserted by her in accordance
with the Copyright, Designs and Patents Act, 1988.
A CIP catalogue record for this book is available
from the British Library.
ISBN 1 84616 323 4
1 3 5 7 9 10 8 6 4 2
Printed in Great Britain

Ruby
the Red
Fairy

by Daisy Meadows

illustrated by Georgie Ripper

ORCHARD BOOKS

The Fairyland Palace

Maze

Forest

Orchard

Black Pot

Meadow

Tower

Beach

Rockpools

Rainspell Island

Jack Frost's
Ice Castle

Tom Goodfellow's
House

Merry-go-round

Mrs Merry's
Cottage

Willow
Tree

Stream

Field

Town

Mermaid
Cottage

Harbour

Dolphin Cottage

Cold winds blow and thick ice form,
I conjure up this fairy storm.
To seven corners of the mortal world
the Rainbow Fairies will be hurled!

I curse every part of Fairyland,
with a frosty wave of my icy hand.
For now and always, from this fateful day,
Fairyland will be cold and grey!

Contents

The End of the Rainbow

"Look, Dad!" said Rachel Walker. She pointed across the blue-green sea at the rocky island ahead of them. The ferry was sailing towards it, dipping up and down on the rolling waves. "Is that Rainspell Island?" she asked.

Her dad nodded. "Yes, it is," he said, smiling. "Our holiday is about to begin!"

The waves slapped against the side
of the ferry as it bobbed up and down
on the water. Rachel felt her heart
thump with excitement. She could see
white cliffs and emerald green fields on
the island. And golden sandy beaches,
with rock pools dotted here and there.

Suddenly, a few fat raindrops
plopped down on to Rachel's head.
"Oh!" she gasped, surprised. The sun
was still shining.

Rachel's mum grabbed her hand. "Let's get under cover," she said, leading Rachel inside.

"Isn't that strange?" Rachel said. "Sunshine *and* rain!"

"Let's hope the rain stops before we get off the ferry," said Mr Walker. "Now, where did I put that map of the island?"

Rachel looked out of the window. Her eyes opened wide.

A girl was standing alone on the deck. Her dark hair was wet with raindrops, but she didn't seem to care. She just stared up at the sky.

Rachel looked over at her mum and dad. They were busy studying the map. So Rachel slipped back outside to see what was so interesting.

And there it was.

In the blue sky, high above them, was the most amazing rainbow that Rachel had ever seen. One end of the rainbow was far out to sea. The other seemed to fall somewhere on Rainspell Island. All of the colours were bright and clear.

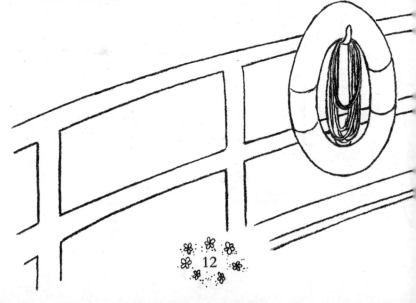

Red,
orange,
yellow,
green,
blue,
indigo
and violet.

"Isn't it perfect?" the dark-haired girl whispered to Rachel.

"Yes, it is," Rachel agreed. "Are you going to Rainspell on holiday?"

The girl nodded. "We're staying for a week," she said. "I'm Kirsty Tate."

Rachel smiled, as the rain began to stop. "I'm Rachel Walker. We're staying at Mermaid Cottage," she added.

"And we're at Dolphin Cottage," said Kirsty. "Do you think we might be near each other?"

"I hope so," Rachel replied. She had a feeling she was going to like Kirsty.

Kirsty leaned over the rail and looked down into the shimmering water. "The sea looks really deep, doesn't it?" she said. "There might even be mermaids down there, watching us right now!"

Rachel stared at the waves. She saw
something that made her heart skip a
beat. "Look!" she said. "Is that a
mermaid's hair?" Then she laughed,
when she saw that it was just seaweed.

"It could be a mermaid's necklace,"
said Kirsty, smiling. "Maybe she lost
it when she was trying to escape from
a sea monster."

The ferry was now sailing into Rainspell's tiny harbour. Seagulls flew around them, and fishing boats bobbed on the water.

"Look at that big white cliff over there," Kirsty said. She pointed it out to Rachel. "It looks a bit like a giant's face, doesn't it?" Rachel looked, and nodded. Kirsty seemed to see magic *everywhere*.

"There you are, Rachel!" called Mrs Walker. Rachel turned round and saw her mum and dad coming out on to the deck. "We'll be getting off the ferry in a few minutes," Mrs Walker added.

"Mum, Dad, this is Kirsty," Rachel said. "She's staying at Dolphin Cottage."

"That's right next door to ours," said Mr Walker. "I remember seeing it on the map."

Rachel and Kirsty looked at each other in delight.

"I'd better go and find *my* mum and dad," said Kirsty. She looked round. "Oh, here they are."

Kirsty's mum and dad came over
to say hello to the Walkers. Then the
ferry docked, and everyone began to
leave the boat.

"Our cottages are on the other side
of the harbour," said Rachel's dad,
looking at the map. "It's not far."

Mermaid Cottage and Dolphin
Cottage were right next to the beach.
Rachel loved her bedroom, which was
high up, in the attic. From the
window, she could see the waves
rolling onto the sand.

A shout from outside made her look down. It was Kirsty. She was standing under the window, waving at her.

"Let's go and explore the beach!" Kirsty called.

Rachel dashed outside to join her.

Seaweed lay in piles on the sand, and there were tiny pink and white shells dotted about.

"I love it here already!" Rachel shouted happily above the noise of the seagulls.

"Me too," Kirsty said. She pointed up at the sky. "Look, the rainbow's still there."

Rachel looked up. The rainbow glowcd brightly among the fluffy white clouds.

"Have you heard the story about the pot of gold at the end of the rainbow?" Kirsty asked.

Rachel nodded. "Yes, but that's just in fairy stories," she said.

Kirsty grinned. "Maybe. But let's go and find out for ourselves!"

"OK," Rachel agreed. "We can explore the island at the same time."

They rushed back to tell their parents
where they were going. Then Kirsty
and Rachel set off along a lane behind
the cottages. It led them away from the
beach, across green fields, and towards
a small wood.

Rachel kept looking up at the rainbow. She was worried that it would start to fade now that the rain had stopped. But the colours stayed clear and bright.

"It looks like the end of the rainbow is over there," Kirsty said. "Come on!" And she hurried towards the trees.

The wood was cool and green after the heat of the sun. Rachel and Kirsty followed a winding path until they came to a clearing. Then they both stopped and stared.

The rainbow shone down on to the grass through a gap in the trees.

And there, at the rainbow's end, lay an old, black pot.

A Tiny Surprise

"Look!" Kirsty whispered. "There really is a pot of gold!"

"It could just be a cooking pot," Rachel said doubtfully. "Some campers might have left it behind."

But Kirsty shook her head. "I don't think so," she said. "It looks really old."

Rachel stared at the pot. It was sitting on the grass, upside down.

"Let's have a closer look," said Kirsty. She ran to the pot and tried to turn it over. "Oh, it's heavy!" she gasped. She tried again, but the pot didn't move.

Rachel rushed to help her. They both pushed and pushed at the pot. This time it moved, just a little.

"Let's try again," Kirsty panted. "Are you ready, Rachel?"

Tap! Tap! Tap!

Rachel and Kirsty stared at each other.

"What was that?" Rachel gasped.

"I don't know," whispered Kirsty.

Tap! Tap!

"There it is again," Kirsty said. She looked down at the pot lying on the grass. "You know what? I think it's coming from inside this pot!"

Rachel's eyes opened wide. "Are you sure?" She bent down, and put her ear to the pot. *Tap! Tap!* Then, to her amazement, Rachel heard a tiny voice.

"Help!" it called. "Help me!"

Rachel grabbed Kirsty's arm. "Did you hear that?" she asked.

Kirsty nodded. "Quick!" she said. "We *must* turn the pot over!"

Rachel and Kirsty pushed at the pot as hard as they could. It began to rock from side to side on the grass.

"We're nearly there!" Rachel panted. "Keep pushing, Kirsty!"

The girls pushed with all their might. Suddenly, the pot turned over and rolled on to its side. Rachel and Kirsty were taken by surprise. They both lost their balance and landed on the grass with a thump.

"Look!" Kirsty whispered, breathing hard.

A small shower of sparkling red dust had flown out of the pot. Rachel and Kirsty gasped with surprise. The dust hung in the air above them. And there, right in the middle of the glittering cloud, was a tiny winged girl.

Rachel and Kirsty watched in wonder as the tiny girl fluttered in the sunlight, her delicate wings sparkling with all the colours of the rainbow.

"Oh, Rachel!" Kirsty whispered. "It's a fairy…"

Fairy Magic

The fairy flew over Rachel and Kirsty's
heads. Her short, silky dress was the
colour of ripe strawberries. Red crystal
earrings glowed in her ears. Her golden
hair was plaited with tiny red roses,
and her little feet wore crimson slippers.

She waved her scarlet wand, and the
shower of sparkling red fairy dust

31

floated softly down to the ground.
Where it landed, all sorts of red flowers
appeared with a *pop!*

Rachel and Kirsty watched
open-mouthed. It really and truly *was*
a fairy.

"This is like a dream," Rachel said.

"I always believed in fairies," Kirsty
whispered back. "But I never thought
I'd ever *see* one!"

The fairy flew towards them. "Oh,
thank you *so* much!" she called in a
tiny, silvery voice. "I'm free at last!"
She glided down, and landed on
Kirsty's hand.

Kirsty gasped. The fairy felt lighter
and softer than a butterfly.

"I was beginning to think I'd *never*
get out of the pot!" the fairy said.

Kirsty wanted to ask the fairy so
many things. But she didn't know
where to start.

"Tell me your names, quickly," said
the fairy. She fluttered up into the air
again. "There's so much to be done,
and we must get started right away."

Rachel wondered what the fairy meant. "I'm Rachel," she said.

"And I'm Kirsty," said Kirsty. "But who are *you?*"

"I'm the Red Rainbow Fairy – but call me Ruby," the fairy replied.

"Ruby..." Kirsty breathed. "A Rainbow Fairy..." She and Rachel stared at each other in excitement. This really *was* magic!

"Yes," said Ruby. "And I have six sisters: Amber, Saffron, Fern, Sky, Izzy and Heather. One for each colour of the rainbow, you see."

"What do Rainbow Fairies do?"
Rachel asked.

Ruby flew over and landed lightly on
Rachel's hand. "It's our job to put all the
different colours into Fairyland," she
explained.

"So why were you shut up inside
that old pot?" asked Rachel.

"And where are your sisters?" Kirsty
added.

Ruby's golden wings drooped. Her
eyes filled with tiny, sparkling tears.
"I don't know," she said. "Something
terrible has happened in Fairyland. We
really need your help!"

Kirsty stared down at Ruby, sitting sadly on Rachel's hand. "Of course we'll help you!" she said.

"Just tell us how," added Rachel.

Ruby wiped the tears from her eyes. "Thank you!" she said. "But first I must show you the terrible thing that has happened. Follow me – as quickly as

you can!" She flew into the air, her
wings shimmering in the
sunshine.

Rachel and Kirsty
followed Ruby across the
clearing. She danced
ahead of them,
glowing like a
crimson flame. She
stopped at a small
pond under a
weeping willow tree.
"Look! I can show
you what happened
yesterday," she said.

She flew over the
pond and scattered another
shower of sparkling fairy dust
with her tiny, red wand. At once,

the water lit up with a strange,
silver light. It bubbled and
fizzed, and then became still.
With wide eyes, Rachel
and Kirsty watched as
a picture appeared.
It was like looking
through a window
into another land!
"Oh, Rachel,
look!" said Kirsty.
A river of
brightest blue ran
swiftly past hills of
greenest green. Scattered
on the hillsides were red
and white toadstool houses.
And on top of the highest hill stood a
silver palace with four pink towers.

The towers were so high, their points were almost hidden by the fluffy white clouds floating past.

Hundreds of fairies were making their way towards the palace. Some were walking and some were flying. Rachel and Kirsty could see goblins, elves, imps and pixies too. Everyone seemed very excited.

"Yesterday was the day of the Fairyland Midsummer Ball," Ruby explained. She flew over the pond and pointed down with her wand to a spot in the middle of the scene. "There I am, with my Rainbow sisters."

Kirsty and Rachel looked closely at where Ruby was pointing. They saw seven fairies, each dressed prettily in their own rainbow colour. Wherever they flew, they left a trail of fairy dust behind them.

"The Midsummer Ball is *very* special," Ruby went on. "And my sisters and I are always in charge of sending out invitations."

To the sound of tinkling music, the front doors of the palace slowly opened.

"Here come King Oberon and Queen Titania," said Ruby. "The Fairy King and Queen. They are about to begin the ball."

Kirsty and Rachel watched as the King and Queen stepped out. The King wore a splendid golden coat and golden crown. His queen wore a silver dress and a tiara that sparkled with diamonds. Everyone cheered loudly. After a while, the King signalled for quiet. "Fairies," he began. "We are very glad to see you all here. Welcome to the Midsummer Ball!"

The fairies clapped their hands and cheered again. A band of green frogs in smart purple outfits started to play, and the dancing began.

Suddenly, a grey mist seemed to fill the room. Kirsty and Rachel watched in alarm as all the fairies started to shiver. And a loud, chilly voice shouted out, "Stop the music!"

The band fell silent. Everyone looked scared. A tall, bony figure was pushing his way through the crowd. He was dressed all in white, and there was frost on his white hair and beard. Icicles hung from his clothes. But his face was red and angry.

"Who's that?" Rachel asked with a shiver. Ice had begun to form around the edge of the pond.

"It's Jack Frost," said Ruby. And she shivered too.

Jack Frost glared at the seven Rainbow Fairies. "Why wasn't I invited to the Midsummer Ball?" he asked coldly.

The Rainbow Fairies gasped in horror...

Ruby looked up from the pond picture. She smiled sadly at Rachel and Kirsty. "Yes, we forgot to invite Jack Frost," she said.

The Fairy Queen stepped forward. "You are very welcome, Jack Frost," she said. "Please stay and enjoy the ball."

But Jack Frost looked even more angry. "Too late!" he hissed. "You forgot to invite me!" He turned and pointed a thin, icy finger at the Rainbow Fairies.

"Well, you will not forget this!" he went on. "My spell will banish the Rainbow Fairies to the seven corners of the mortal world. From this day on, Fairyland will be without colour – for ever!"

Jack Frost's Spell

As Jack Frost cast his spell, a great, icy wind began to blow. It picked up the seven Rainbow Fairies and spun them up into the darkening sky. The other fairies watched in dismay.

Jack Frost turned to the King and Queen. "Your Rainbow Fairies will be trapped, never to return." With that, he left, leaving a trail of icy footprints.

Quickly, the Fairy Queen stepped forward and lifted her silver wand. "I cannot undo Jack Frost's magic completely," she shouted, as the wind howled and rushed around her. "But I can guide the Rainbow Fairies to a safe place until they can be rescued!"

The Queen pointed her wand at the

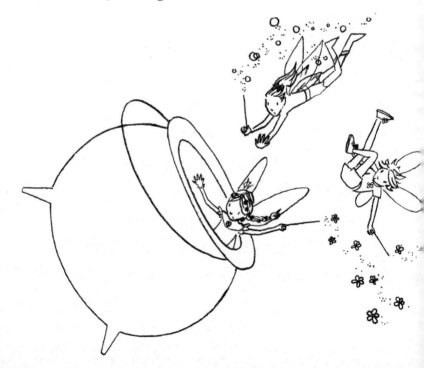

grey sky overhead. A black pot came spinning through the stormy clouds. It flew towards the Rainbow Fairies. One by one, the Rainbow Fairies tumbled into the pot.

"Pot-at-the-end-of-the-rainbow, keep our Rainbow Fairies safely together," the Queen called. "And take them to Rainspell Island!"

The pot flew out of sight, behind a dark cloud. And the bright colours of Fairyland began to fade, until it looked like an old black and white photograph.

"Oh no!" Kirsty gasped. Then the picture in the pond vanished.

"So the Fairy Queen cast her *own* spell!" Rachel said. She was bursting with questions. "She put you and your sisters in the pot, and sent you to Rainspell."

Ruby nodded. "Our Queen knew that we would be safe here," she said. "We know Rainspell well. It is a place full of magic."

"But where are your sisters?" Kirsty wanted to know. "They were in the pot too."

Ruby looked upset. "Jack Frost's spell must have been stronger than the Queen thought," she said. "As the pot spun through the sky, the wind blew my sisters out again. I was at the bottom, so I was safe. But I was trapped when the pot landed upside down."

"So are your sisters somewhere on Rainspell?" Kirsty asked.

Ruby nodded. "Yes, but they're scattered all over the island. Jack Frost's spell has trapped them too." She flew towards Kirsty and landed on her shoulder. "That's where you and Rachel come in."

"How?" Rachel asked.

"You found *me*, didn't you?" the fairy went on. "That's because you believe in magic." She flew from Kirsty's shoulder to Rachel's. "So, you could rescue my Rainbow sisters too! Then we can all bring colour back to Fairyland again."

A Visit to Fairyland

"Of course we'll search for your sisters," Kirsty said quickly. "Won't we, Rachel?"

Rachel nodded.

"Oh, thank you," Ruby said happily.

"But we're only here for a week," Rachel said. "Will that be long enough?"

"We must get started right away,"

said Ruby. "First, I must take you to
Fairyland to meet our King and
Queen. They will be very pleased to
know that you are going to help me
find my sisters."

Rachel and Kirsty stared at Ruby.

"You're taking us to *Fairyland?*"
Kirsty gasped. She could hardly believe
her ears. Nor could Rachel.

"But how will we get there?" Rachel
wanted to know.

"We'll fly there," Ruby replied.

"But *we* can't fly!" Rachel pointed
out.

Ruby smiled. She whirled up into
the air and flew over the girls'
heads. Then she swirled her wand
above them. Magic red fairy dust
fluttered down.

Rachel and Kirsty began to feel a bit strange. Were the trees getting bigger or were they getting smaller?

They were getting smaller!

Smaller and smaller and smaller, until they were the same size as Ruby.

"I'm tiny!" Rachel laughed. She was so small, the flowers around her seemed like trees.

Kirsty twisted round to look at her back. She had wings – shiny and delicate as a butterfly's! Ruby beamed at them. "Now you can fly," she said. "Let's go."

Rachel twitched her shoulders. Her wings fluttered, and she felt herself rise up into the air. She felt quite wobbly at first. It was very odd!

"Help!" Kirsty yelled, as she shot up into the air. "I'm not very good at this!"

"Come on," said Ruby, taking their hands. "I'll help you." She led them up, out of the glade.

Rachel looked down on Rainspell Island. She could see the cottages next to the beach, and the harbour.

"Where *is* Fairyland, Ruby?" Kirsty asked. They were flying higher and higher, up into the clouds.

"It's so far away, that no mortal could ever find it," Ruby said.

They flew on through the clouds for a long, long time. But at last Ruby turned to them and smiled. "We're here," she said.

As they flew down from the clouds, Kirsty and Rachel saw places they recognised from the pond picture: the palace, the hillsides with their toadstool houses, the river and flowers. But there were no bright colours now. Because of Jack Frost's spell, everything was a drab shade of grey. Even the air felt cold and damp.

A few fairies walked miserably across the hillsides. Their wings hung limply down their backs. No one could be bothered to fly.

Suddenly, one of the fairies looked up into the sky. "Look!" she shouted. "It's Ruby. She's come back!"

At once, the fairies flew up towards
Ruby, Kirsty and Rachel. They circled
around them, looking much happier,
and asking lots of questions.

"Have you come from Rainspell,
Ruby?"

"Where are the other Rainbow
Fairies?"

"Who are your friends?"

"First, we must see the King and
Queen. Then I will tell you
everything!" Ruby promised.

King Oberon and Queen Titania were seated on their thrones. Their palace was as grey and gloomy as everywhere else in Fairyland. But they smiled warmly when Ruby arrived with Rachel and Kirsty.

"Welcome back, Ruby," the Queen said. "We have missed you."

"Your Majesties, I have found two mortals who believe in magic!" Ruby announced. "These are my friends, Kirsty and Rachel."

Quickly Ruby explained what had happened to the other Rainbow Fairies. She told everyone how Rachel and Kirsty had rescued her.

"You have our thanks," the King told them. "Our Rainbow Fairies are very special to us."

"And will you help us to find Ruby's Rainbow sisters?" the Queen asked.

"Yes, we will," Kirsty said.

"But how will we know where to look?" Rachel wanted to know.

"The trick is not to look too hard," said Queen Titania. "Don't worry. As you enjoy the rest of your holiday, the magic you need to find each Rainbow Fairy will find *you*. Just wait and see."

King Oberon rubbed his beard thoughtfully. "You have six days of your holiday left, and six fairies to find," he said. "A fairy each day. That's a lot of fairy-finding. You will need some special help." He nodded at one of his footmen, a plump frog in a buttoned-up jacket.

The frog hopped over to Rachel and Kirsty and handed them each a tiny, silver bag.

"The bags contain magic tools," the Queen told them. "Don't look inside them yet. Open them only when you really need to, and you will find something to help you." She smiled at Kirsty and Rachel.

"Look!" shouted another frog footman suddenly. "Ruby is beginning to fade!"

Rachel and Kirsty looked at Ruby in horror. The fairy was growing paler before their eyes. Her lovely dress was no longer red but pink, and her golden hair was turning white.

"Jack Frost's magic is still at work," said the King, looking worried. "We cannot undo his spell until the Rainbow Fairies are all together again."

"Quickly, Ruby!" urged the Queen. "You must return to Rainspell at once."

Ruby, Kirsty and Rachel rose into the air, their wings fluttering.

"Don't worry!" Kirsty called, as they flew higher. "We'll be back with all the Rainbow Fairies very soon!"

"Good luck!" called the King and Queen.

Rachel and Kirsty watched Ruby worriedly as they flew off. But as they got further away from Fairyland, Ruby's colour began to return. Soon she was bright and sparkling again.

They reached Rainspell at last. Ruby led Rachel and Kirsty to the clearing in the wood, and they landed next to the old, black pot. Then Ruby scattered fairy dust over Rachel and Kirsty. There was a puff of glittering red smoke, and the two girls shot up to their normal size again. Rachel wriggled her shoulders. Yes, her wings had gone. "Oh, I really *loved* being a fairy," Kirsty said.

They watched as Ruby sprinkled her magic dust over the old, black pot.

"What are you doing?" Rachel asked.

"Jack Frost's magic means that I can't help you look for my sisters," Ruby replied sadly. "So I will wait for you here, in the pot-at-the-end-of-the-rainbow."

Suddenly the pot began to move. It rolled across the grass, and stopped under the weeping willow tree. The tree's branches hung right down to the ground.

"The pot will be hidden under the tree," Ruby explained. "I'll be safe there."

"We'd better start looking for the other Rainbow Fairies," Rachel said to Kirsty. "Where shall we start?"

Ruby shook her head. "Remember what the Queen said," she told them. "The magic will come to you." She flew over and sat on the edge of the pot. Then she pushed aside one of the willow branches and waved at Rachel and Kirsty. "Goodbye, and good luck!"

"We'll be back soon, Ruby," Kirsty promised.

"We're going to find all your Rainbow sisters," Rachel said firmly. "Just you wait and see!"

Ruby is safely hidden in the
pot-at-the-end-of-the-rainbow.
Now Rachel and Kirsty must find

Amber the Orange Fairy

A Very Unusual Shell

"What a lovely day!" Rachel Walker shouted, staring up at the blue sky. She and her friend, Kirsty Tate, were running along Rainspell Island's yellow, sandy beach. Their parents walked a little way behind them.

"It's a *magical* day," Kirsty added. The two friends smiled at each other.

Rachel and Kirsty had come to Rainspell Island for their holidays. They had soon found out it really *was* a magical place!

As they ran, they passed rock pools that shone like jewels in the sunshine.

Rachel spotted a little *splash!* in one of the pools. "There's something in there, Kirsty!" she pointed. "Let's go and look."

The girls jogged over to the pool and crouched down to see.

Kirsty's heart thumped as she gazed into the crystal clear water. "What is it?" she asked.

Suddenly, the water rippled. A little brown crab scuttled sideways across the sandy bottom and vanished under a rock.

Kirsty felt disappointed. "I thought it might be another Rainbow Fairy," she said.

"So did I, "Rachel sighed. "Never mind. We'll keep on looking."

"Of course we will," Kirsty agreed. Then she put her finger to her lips as their parents came up behind them. "*Ssh.*"

Kirsty and Rachel had a big secret. They were helping to find the Rainbow Fairies. Thanks to Jack Frost's wicked spell, the fairies were lost on Rainspell Island. And until they were all found there would be no colour in Fairyland.

Rachel looked at the shimmering blue sea. "Shall we have a swim?" she asked.

But Kirsty wasn't listening. She was shading her eyes with her hand and looking further along the beach. "Over there, Rachel – by those rocks," she said.

Then Rachel could see it too – something winking and sparkling in the sunshine. "Wait for me!" she called, as Kirsty hurried over there.

When they saw what it was, the two friends sighed in disappointment.

"It's just the wrapper from a chocolate bar," Rachel said sadly. She bent down and picked up the shiny purple foil.

Kirsty thought for a moment. "Do you remember what the Fairy Queen said?" she asked.

Rachel nodded. *"Let the magic come to*

you," she said. "You're right, Kirsty. We should just enjoy our holiday, and wait for the magic to happen."

Read the rest of

Amber the Orange Fairy

to find out what magic happens next...

RAINBOW magic

by Daisy Meadows

Ruby the Red Fairy ISBN 1 84362 016 2
She's all alone on Rainspell Island...until Rachel and Kirsty
promise to track down her Rainbow sisters.

Amber the Orange Fairy ISBN 1 84362 017 0
She's trapped tight in an unusual place. Can a fluffy feather
help rescue her?

Saffron the Yellow Fairy ISBN 1 84362 018 9
She's stuck in a very sticky situation. How will Rachel and
Kirsty free her?

Fern the Green Fairy ISBN 1 84362 019 7
She's lost in a leafy hollow. And there's a secret to solve to
save her.

Sky the Blue Fairy ISBN 1 84362 020 0
She's having some bubble trouble. Can the rainbow-coloured
crab help?

Izzy the Indigo Fairy ISBN 1 84362 021 9
She's up to her usual mischief. Rachel and Kirsty must get her
back to the pot...before it's too late.

Heather the Violet Fairy ISBN 1 84362 022 7
She's in a spin. Until the colourful carousel horses rush to
her rescue.

All priced at £3.99
Rainbow Magic books are available from all good bookshops,
or can be ordered direct from the publisher:
Orchard Books, PO BOX 29, Douglas IM99 1BQ
Credit card orders please telephone 01624 836000
or fax 01624 837033 or visit our Internet site: www.wattspub.co.uk
or e-mail: bookshop@enterprise.net for details.

To order please quote title, author and ISBN
and your full name and address.
Cheques and postal orders should be made payable to 'Bookpost plc.'
Postage and packing is FREE within the UK
(overseas customers should add £1.00 per book).

Prices and availability are subject to change.